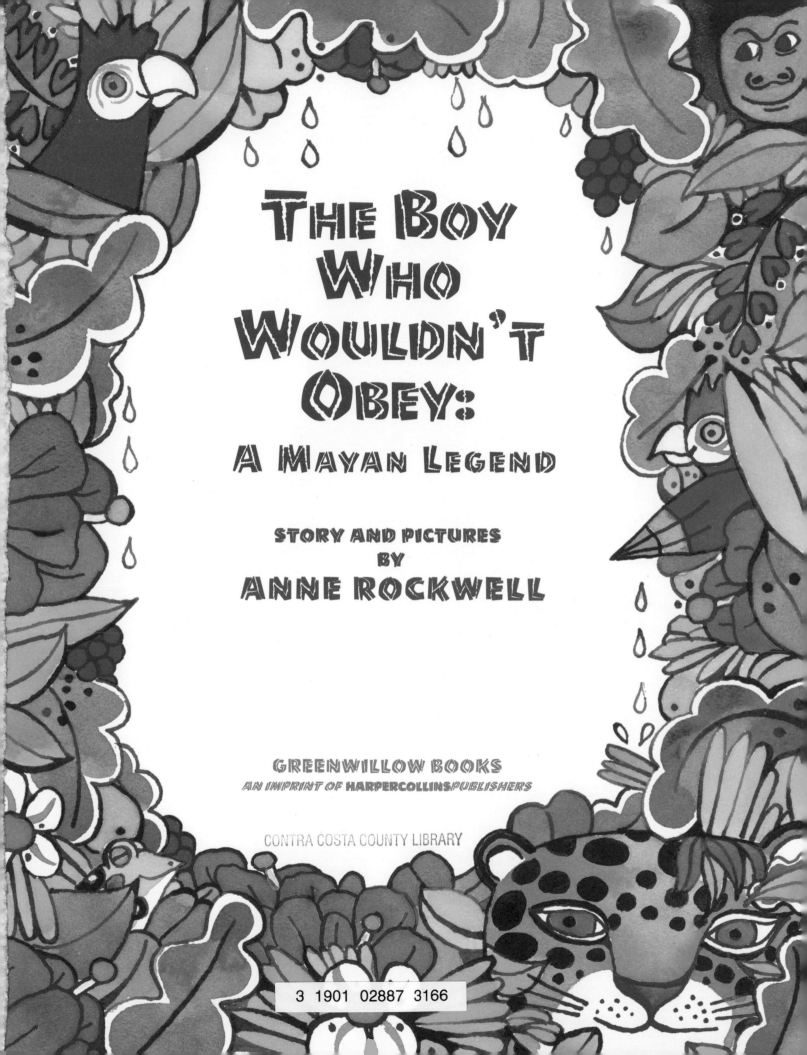

The Boy Who Wouldn't Obey:
A Mayan Legend

STORY AND PICTURES
BY
ANNE ROCKWELL

GREENWILLOW BOOKS
AN IMPRINT OF HARPERCOLLINSPUBLISHERS

For Nicholas, Nigel,
and Christian,
who all like legends

The Boy Who Wouldn't Obey was adapted from "Chac" in *The Monkey's Haircut and Other Stories Told by the Maya*, edited by John Bierhorst, copyright © 1986 by John Bierhorst, by permission of the publisher, Morrow Junior Books, a division of William Morrow & Company, Inc.

Pen and ink and watercolors were used for the full-color art.
The text type is Bernhard Modern BT.

The Boy Who Wouldn't Obey: A Mayan Legend
Copyright © 2000 by Anne Rockwell
Printed in Hong Kong by South China Printing Company (1988) Ltd.
All rights reserved.
http://www.harperchildrens.com

Library of Congress Cataloging-in-Publication Data

Rockwell, Anne F.
The boy who wouldn't obey : a Mayan legend / story and pictures by Anne Rockwell.
p.   cm.
"Greenwillow Books."
Summary: When Chac, the great lord who makes rain,
takes a disobedient boy as his servant, they are both in for trouble.
ISBN 0-688-14881-6
1. Mayas—Folklore.   2. Tales—Mexico.   [1. Mayas—Folklore.
2. Indians of Mexico—Folklore.   3. Folklore—Mexico.]   I. Title.
F1435.3.F6R65   2000   398.2'089'97415—dc21   99-15201   CIP

1 2 3 4 5 6 7 8 9 10   First Edition

FOREWORD

Modern Mayans of Central America are descendants of people who created
a civilization that had collapsed before the Spanish conquistador Hernando
Cortés sailed to Mexico in the sixteenth century. The reason for this collapse
is one of the great mysteries of history. When I visited Mayan ruins on the
Yucatán peninsula in Mexico, I was awed to see ancient pyramids rising above
the trees. I wanted to learn more about the people who had built them.

The Mayans invented a system of hieroglyphic writing and created beautiful
illustrated manuscripts containing their sacred literature. But the conquistadors
feared what was written in these manuscripts and destroyed most of them.
Fortunately, many ceramic vessels covered with images and writing survived.
These were the inspiration for my illustrations.

The Mayans believed in numerous gods who created humans for only one
purpose—to serve them. Among them were four named Chac. Each Chac
ruled one of the corners of the vast square that the Mayans believed formed
earth and sky, controlling the rain, wind, thunder, and lightning that came
from his corner. In art, Chacs have human bodies and wear the jade-and-shell
jewelry of a Mayan noble, but their blue bodies are covered with reptilian scales.
They have the long, curling whiskers of a catfish and the wide mouth of a frog.
Their noses are unlike those of any other creature.

Again and again in Mayan art, certain animals of the Central American
rain forest—the jaguar, macaw, and monkey—appear. Mayan mythology says
it was a monkey who first wrote down stories. That's why on each text page I've
included a monkey scribe observing and recording what happens.

Scholars today are learning to decipher Mayan writing. Sky is represented
by a band containing symbols of clouds, rain, thunder and lightning, stars and
planets. Since most of this story takes place above the clouds, I've adapted a
sky band as a motif on each text page. Next to my signature below is my
adaptation of the symbol for drawing, painting, and writing—which to the
Mayans were all the same thing.

Chac, the great lord who made rain, lived high above the clouds in a fine house with a beautiful garden.

He didn't spend much time at home. Every day he traveled to wherever the sun blazed hot and the earth was dry. He poured rain onto the parched plants from a gourd that was never empty. This was the good thing Chac did.

But he also liked to cause trouble. Often he opened his leather bag of winds and let them blow, just for the fun of it. Chac laughed when he saw the winds blow the roofs off people's houses or topple their trees. In case anyone still doubted his power, he would hurl his ax across the sky to make lightning and beat his drum to make thunder. Whoever saw the lightning and heard the thunder ran for shelter.

Everyone was afraid of Chac, even Monkey, who knew all the stories that told how everything in the world came to be.

One day Chac decided he needed a servant. He dived down to a forest, where a boy sat listening to Monkey tell stories.

Neither the boy nor Monkey saw Chac coming. They couldn't, for the lord of rain was as blue as the morning sky, and his clothes were as green as the leaves that sprout in the forest after rain falls.

Chac grabbed the boy and carried him to his home in the sky. "From now on, you must do whatever I tell you to do," he said.

Unfortunately, Chac didn't know that the boy he'd stolen rarely did what he was told. In fact, that very morning the boy's father had told him to help his brother catch some fish for dinner. But instead the boy had run off to the forest to hear Monkey's stories.

So when Chac told the boy he must never use the jade shovel he kept in his garden, the boy disobeyed him, too. As soon as Chac was out of sight, he took the shovel and began to dig. He dug and dug all day. He made a hole in the sky, and soon he could see his mother, his father, and his brother searching for him.

"Here I am!" the boy called, but they couldn't hear him calling to them from beyond the clouds.

He was very sad and wanted to go home. He tied one end of a long rope to a tree. He grabbed hold of the other end and began to let himself down through the clouds. But the rope wasn't long enough. It didn't come anywhere near the earth.

When Chac saw the boy dangling in the sky, he was very angry.
He opened his bag, and winds began to blow.

The boy spun around and around until he was dizzy. His hands
stung from holding the rope, and he knew he couldn't hold on
much longer. He begged Chac to make the winds stop, but Chac
just made them blow harder.

Finally Chac decided he wanted dinner. He told the winds to
stop, pulled the boy up through the sky, and scolded him harshly.
Then he set him to work grinding corn, cutting squash, shucking
beans, cooking and serving dinner, and washing dishes. He sent the
boy to bed with nothing to eat.

The next morning he ordered his servant to pick some ripe corn
from his garden and grind it for bread. The boy did—enough corn
to make bread for two—but Chac didn't share his bread.

As the hungry boy watched Chac eat, the lord of rain shouted, "Ha! I know what you're thinking! Don't you dare pick a single ear of corn from my garden!"

But no sooner was Chac out of sight than the boy ran outside and reached for the most golden ear of corn growing on Chac's tallest cornstalk.

At that very moment the ax came flying through the air. It missed the boy but hit the cornstalk. Lightning sizzled. Chac's finest cornstalk fell to the ground.

That night, when Chac came home, he punished the boy so severely that he cried and promised he'd never disobey his master again.

And he didn't. In fact, he became quite a good servant who always worked hard to please his master. He tried not to think of his family far away.

One day Chac said, "Clean my house. Cook something delicious. Make sure everything is perfect, because I've invited guests for dinner."

The boy did exactly as he was told. He cleaned the house and polished the furniture and set the table with Chac's best dishes. He mopped the floor until it shone, made a delicious stew, and set it on the fire to cook. Then he went outside to cut fresh flowers for the table.

When he returned to the house, he was horrified to see a great many frogs sitting on the clean, polished table. Puddles of water were all over the floor.

"Get out!" he shouted, and chased the frogs away. He began to mop up the puddles as fast as he could. But he wasn't fast enough.

Chac came home and shouted, "Why are you still mopping the floor, you lazy boy?"

"I cleaned all day and made everything look beautiful," the boy said sadly. "But lots of slimy frogs got inside and dripped water everywhere. Don't worry, Master—I chased them away."

"Oh—you stupid, stupid boy!" Chac shouted. "Those were my dinner guests. Haven't you heard the frogs singing to me when I make rain? I wanted to give a party to thank them."

Again Chac punished his servant boy, more cruelly than ever before.

That night the boy lay awake, trying to think of a way to get even. At last he did. While the great lord of rain was sleeping, the boy stole his leather bag, his water gourd, his ax, and his drum.

"You'd better stop being mean to me if you want these back!" he muttered, as Chac slept on.

The boy ran outside. He untied the strings that held the bag
tightly closed. As soon as he did, wild winds escaped and blew
across the sky.

"Come back!" the boy commanded in a voice he thought
sounded every bit as stern and cruel as Chac's.

But the winds only wailed, blew harder, and wouldn't obey.

He threw Chac's ax toward them. "Go get them!" he
commanded.

But the ax didn't obey him either. Lightning sizzled and
flashed along the ax's path.

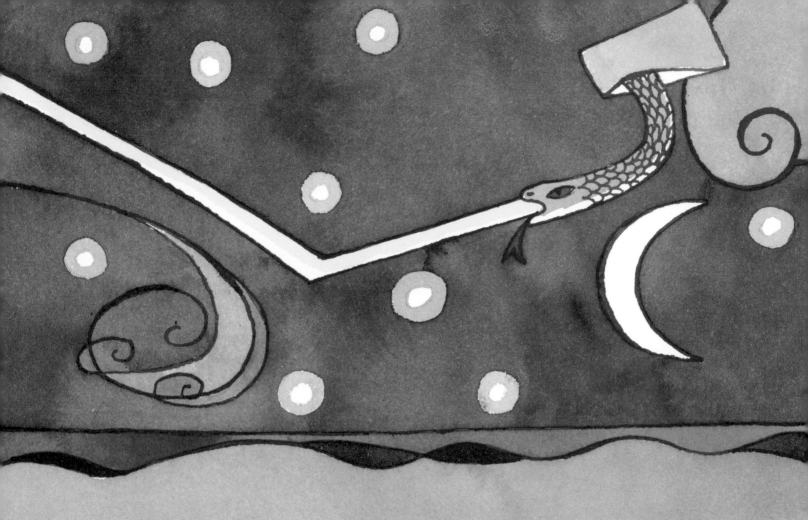

The boy ran after the ax, but as he did, rain spilled from the
gourd. Floods poured down. The rain didn't stop, for the gourd was
never empty, and only great Chac knew how to make it stop pouring.

The boy beat hard on the drum. The drum boomed with thunder.
But the winds kept blowing, the gourd kept pouring, and the ax
danced faster and faster.

By now the boy was terrified at what he'd done. He ran across
the sky, begging wind and rain, thunder and lightning to stop. But
they didn't.

He ran faster, then stumbled and fell into the sea.

When Chac woke up and saw that his rain-making tools and his servant were gone, he guessed what had happened. He commanded wind and rain, thunder and lightning to stop, and they did. Far below, he saw the boy struggling to stay afloat in the waves of the sea.

"I suppose you're going to beg me to take pity on you and bring you back!" Chac shouted. "Well, I won't! I don't want you for my servant. You disobey and steal! Go back where you came from!"

As soon as Chac said that, a gust of wind blew the boy across the sea, home to where his mother and father and brother were cleaning up the trees that lay uprooted in their yard.

They were very, very happy to see him.

"What a storm we had last night!" his brother said. "I know it would have scared you, because it scared me. I thought the wind would blow our house away! It was the worst storm we've ever had!"

The boy had always wanted to do something his big brother couldn't. "I caused that terrible storm, all by myself!" he said proudly.

Of course his brother didn't believe him.

But Monkey did. He had seen every single thing that happened to the boy who had been great Chac's servant, and he wrote it all down.

That's how we know this story is true.

NOTE ON THE SOURCES

I've referred to many books on Mayan civilization and art and looked at ceramic collections in numerous museums—especially the beautiful examples in the Museum of Fine Arts, Boston; the Metropolitan Museum of Art, New York; and the American Museum of Natural History, New York.

Books I've found particularly helpful are:

Painting the Maya Universe: Royal Ceramics of the Classic Period, by Doris Reents-Budet with contributions by Joseph W. Ball, Ronald L. Bishop, Virginia M. Fields, and Barbara MacLeod, photographs by Justin Kerr (Durham, NC: Duke University Press, 1994).

Popul Vuh: The Mayan Book of the Dawn of Life, Revised Edition, translated by Dennis Tedlock (New York: Simon & Schuster, 1996).

The Blood of Kings: Dynasty and Ritual in Maya Art, by Linda Schele and Mary Ellen Miller, photographs by Justin Kerr (New York: George Braziller, Inc., in association with Kimball Art Museum, Fort Worth, TX, 1986).

An Illustrated Dictionary of the Gods and Symbols of Ancient Mexico and the Maya, by Mary Miller and Karl Taube (London: Thames and Hudson, 1963).

Maya, edited by Peter Schmidt, Mercedes de la Garza, and Enrique Nalda (New York: Rizzoli International Publications, Inc., 1998).